For Princess Lucy Lisle

CONTENTS

1

Princesses Don't Do Dirt

Molly worked on Hill Farm in the muck.

But she wanted to be a princess.

She milked the cows and goats.

She tugged up tough turnips and

stubborn swedes. She fed the chickens –
the mice too.

But she dreamed of being a princess.

She scratched the grumpy old pigs. She
stroked the sheep and spun their wool into
cloth.

She fed and groomed the dusty donkey,
though he always tried to kick her.

Molly lived on the farm with her ma and

pa. They were poor farmers, always dreaming of a better life.

'You'd make a perfect princess!' Ma said. 'You're such a lovely girl!'

Molly had long wavy blonde hair right down to her knees. She had big brown eyes . . .

'You've got such a teeny tiny waist. Your

nose is so sweet!' Pa said. 'It's not right you should work your fingers to the bone on this old farm.'

'The only thing wrong with you is those big things,' Ma said, pointing at Molly's enormous feet.

'Don't!' Molly quickly tucked them out of sight beneath her dress. 'Thank goodness Stan doesn't mind my feet,' she said.

Stan was a blacksmith. He lived on the

next hill. He was very good at making things. He was kind and had lovely blue eyes. But he was not a prince.

And Molly wanted a prince because princesses had princes.

2

Preparing to be a Real Princess

One day, a notice was pinned up in the village square.

~ Prince Seeks Princess ~
Must be of highest quality and prove herself PERFECT in every way.
Princesses must present themselves at the Royal Palace for Testing
Saturday, 12th July 4pm.

Molly jumped for joy. Ma did a jig.

'This is your chance!' Ma cried. 'You'll marry the Prince and we'll get rich and get rid of the farm. Yipee!'

Stan was worried and shook his head sadly.

Ma went to the library and took out some books. *Sleeping Beauty. The Princess and the Pea. Cinderella. Snow White and the Seven Dwarves.* They were so heavy Ma had to put them in the back of Stan's cart to get them home.

'It's all here,' said Ma, tapping the books. 'All the clues you need are in these books. All the tricks and scams to make you a perfect princess. Listen, you must:

Feel the Royal Pea Under the Mattresses.

Show you can Dance all Night until Your Slippers Wear Out.

Avoid Spinning Wheels. Avoid Evil Stepmothers. Be Nice to Older Women in Case They Turn out to be Evil Stepmothers or Witches.

Be Kind and Helpful to all Dwarves Especially if there are Seven of them.'

'What a lot of things to remember!' cried Molly.

'Are you sure you want to be a princess?' Stan asked her quietly. 'Sounds like a waste of time to me.'

'Oh, yes.' Molly said. 'More than anything in the world.'

Stan sighed and shook his head.

'Now,' Ma said. 'You need a princess's name!'

'What's wrong with Molly?' Stan asked.

'It's dreadful! Can't think how we chose it. Dull and unprincessy . . . ' Ma flicked through the Dictionary of Princess Names. 'Annabellabella, Arabellabella . . . Pansy, Pinsey, Ponsey . . . These are all horrible. Ah, Blondine!' Ma cried. 'Princess Blondine is a smashing name for you.'

'Is it?' Molly said. 'Blondine is a very pretty name but I don't have the clothes to match.'

'True,' Ma said. 'You'll need a ballgown for the ball and glass slippers too! Hmmm, no fairy godmothers around, are there?' She peered over the sides of the cart hopefully. 'No. Well, I'll have to get out Grandma's old wedding dress and we'll royal it up.'

'You'll look wonderful whatever you wear,' said Stan.

Stan didn't want Molly to be a princess. He loved her the way she was.

The next time he came to see her, Stan brought her a present. It was hundreds of tiny sparkling things to sew on her dress. They were minuscule bits of silvery scrap metal, fragments of mirror – everything he could find in his workshop. He had made her a crown too.

Ma had bought Molly two pairs of slippers: one pair to wear during the day and the other pair for the ball.

'They're special. I spent all our savings on them,' Ma told Molly. 'You and your great big feet!'

'Thank you, Ma. I'll try and win,' Molly said. 'But I don't think I'll ever remember all the things I have to do.'

'Nonsense!' Ma said. 'There'll be a way round it. You don't believe princesses are any different to us, do you?' Her eyes glinted. 'I bet they all cheat!'

3

The Princesses in the Palace

Molly went to say goodbye to the farm animals. She took her slippers and Stan's crown to show them.

'Goodbye, friends,' she said. 'I'll miss you.'

She scratched the pigs. She fed the hens

(and the mice). She gave the goats and the donkey some turnip tops. But the goats poked their head through the fence and ate her new slippers. Much tastier than turnip tops!

'Oh! You bad things!' Molly cried. 'You naughty goats. Now I'll have to wear my clogs like any old peasant! Those slippers were so expensive! Specially made for me. Oh, I shan't miss you!'

Stan took Molly to the palace in his donkey and cart. Molly asked him to leave her where no one could see the wobbly old cart or hear his donkey braying.

'I hope you win, Molly,' said Stan,

'because you want to, but . . . Oh, never mind. Goodbye!' He drove away, adding under his breath, 'You'll always be a real princess to me.'

There were princesses everywhere. They all had long hair down to their knees, gorgeous dresses, beautiful noses, tiny waists and even worse . . . tiny feet . . .

Molly hid her scruffy wooden clogs beneath her skirt. (Naughty goats!) She

tossed her hair back and set out to walk up the drive to the palace.

A carriage went by. Inside was Princess Esmeralda. She had fiery red hair and green eyes. There were emeralds all over her dress. She sneered at Molly as if Molly was covered in boils and spots.

'I'll show you!' Molly thought. 'I'll have the last sneer!'

At last she reached the palace.

There was a man at the door wearing the most heavenly clothes made of satin and silk. He smelled of rose water and lavender.

'Good afternoon, princess,' he said, bowing.

'Hello, King,' Molly said.

The princesses giggled. 'He's the butler,

you twit!'

'Of course I know he is,' said Molly. She lifted her chin up and looked down her nose at the butler. 'I was just joking.'

'Papers!' said the butler.

Molly handed over her papers.

Princess Blondine of the Country of Mollyakiya.

She had spent hours working on the documents. She had aged the papers by soaking them in lemon juice then baking them in the oven till the edges browned.

'Pass,' said the butler.

Molly grinned. That was the first test! And she'd passed!

She picked up her bags.

'What are you doing?' squeaked Princess Snowflake. 'Leave them for your footman and your maid!'

Molly paused. Of course she didn't have a footman or a maid.

'Unfortunately,' she said, slowly, 'we had a battle last week in Mollyakiya with a very large dragon. The entire staff was grilled to a crisp.'

'Oooh! How exciting.' Princess Snowflake shivered. Her white-blonde hair rippled. 'I wish we had dragons! How thrilling!'

'Yes, very,' said Molly. She swept inside with her bags.

Molly was in a great hall with pillars and

mirrors. Chandeliers as big as cows dangled from the ceiling. There were lots and lots of princesses . . . and some were already leaving!

'It's not fair,' said Princess Marybellabella as she pushed past Molly. 'How was I supposed to know that horrible, stinky little man was one of the seven dwarves?' She went out sobbing into her lace hanky.

The same small man approached Molly. He had a very pink face, a snouty nose and a white beard. He was snorting and spitting and s t a m p i n g his feet. He r e m i n d e d Molly of her pigs.

'Hello, charmingly small person,' said Molly. She kissed his lumpy nose and scratched him briefly behind his pointed ear, just like she did to the pigs.

The grumpy dwarf made a happy snorting noise and shivered with pleasure.

'Pass, Princess!' he yelled.

Molly went through the wide golden doors.

She had got through test number two!

4

Putting the Princesses through their Paces

Molly found herself in a massive room with a blue marble floor. She was introduced to the real King and Queen. The King was small and quiet. The Queen was tall with a very loud voice. The Prince was not there.

25

'Prince Percy Percival is far too busy to meet all you gals!' the Queen bellowed. 'He will attend the ball tonight and will dance with the remaining princesses left in the competition.'

Fifty princesses had started the competition; now there were forty-two.

They giggled and chatted like a flock of parrots in the treetops. Molly tried to join in, but they were talking about handbags and lace and Sir thingy this and Lord thingy that; subjects she knew nothing about. The only thing she could think about to discuss was her hens and the naughty goats back at the

farm. And Stan. She missed Stan a lot.

The Queen clapped her hands to get their attention.

'There is something in the next room that I want you all to see,' said the Queen. 'Follow me in groups of ten, please.'

'I wonder what the test is?' Princess Esmeralda asked Molly. 'Do you think it will be matching nail colour varnish to handbags? I'm good at that. Or what to wear on the beach? Which is the best mascara? Isn't this fun? I do hope I win!'

You'd win the Daftest Twit Competition without trying, Molly thought.

They went into the little room. Sunshine slanted in through one small window onto the wooden object placed there.

The other princesses ran up to the wooden thing. They shrieked. They flapped and cooed.

'Oh, isn't it lovely!'

'Isn't it quaint?'

'What can it be?'

'It's one of those things to help you mount a horse!'

'No, it's an exercise machine!'

Molly knew what it was. She didn't say anything. She watched as eight of the silly things, one after the other, pricked their fingers on the sharp spindle.

'Ouch!'

'Ow!'

'It bit me!'

'Failed. Failed. Failed,' the Queen said firmly. She crossed the princesses' names off her list, one by one.

'You next, Princess Blondine.'

'It's a spinning wheel,' Molly said to the Queen. 'Our peasants have them in the village. You spin wool on them . . . I believe.'

'Oh, yes, it's a spinning wheel,' said Princess Esmeralda. She had never seen one before so she just copied Molly.

'Excellent! You two have passed and can

go—' She paused. She'd just noticed Molly's clogs. 'Ugh!' She frowned. 'Princess Blondine! Why are you wearing those clumsy wooden clogs?'

Molly looked down at her feet. She blushed. Bother the goats!

'I do apologise,' she said, sweetly. 'But there have been so many balls lately! I have

danced and danced and danced! I've worn out every single pair of my slippers. My daddy, the King of Mollyakiya, said he wouldn't buy me any more.'

'Excellent!' said the Queen. 'Excellent!' She beamed at Molly. 'I do like a gal with spirit!'

Molly smiled sweetly. Another two tests passed!

5
Sleeping On It

GALS!

After the spinning-wheel test, the remaining twenty-two princesses gathered in the blue marble room again.

'Gals!' The Queen clapped her hands. 'Before tonight's ball you will all have a rest.'

Molly and the other princesses went up the grand staircase to a large bedroom where twenty-two beds were piled high with a multitude of brightly coloured mattresses.

The PEA test! Molly trembled. How was she ever going to know if there was a pea under all those mattresses? Her bed at home was as hard as a plank – in fact it was a plank!

The other princesses weren't worried. They took off their crowns, slipped off their shoes and lay down.

Molly tossed and twizzled and got in a tangle with her sheets. Was there a pea beneath her or not? Yes? No! Yes? No!

Squeak, squeak. A mouse appeared beside her.

'Dear mouse,' said Molly, 'please help me! There are lots of mice on our farm; I feed them when I feed the hens. Please would

you look under my mattress and see if there
is a pea there? You may eat it if you find one.'

'Cool,' the mouse said. He squeezed
between the lower mattresses and after a
scuffling and scratching, appeared with a pea
in his mouth.

'Thanks,' said the mouse and scuttled

away.

Another test passed. Molly could sleep at last.

Two hours later, the Queen came to wake them up.

'Did you sleep well?' she asked.

'Oh, yes, thank you,' said Princess Gloriabella. 'Heavenly.'

'Hah! I knew you weren't a real princess. A real princess would have felt that pea! You have failed,' said the Queen. 'Out you go. OUT!'

'I couldn't sleep a wink,' said Princess Bellabella. 'There was something in my bed, something hard and round and so annoying!'

'Rubbish,' the Queen snapped. 'Your mattresses were perfect. You've failed. There is the door!'

The Queen turned to Molly.

Molly showed her a big bruise on her leg.

'Oh, your Majesty,' she wailed. 'There was

something so hard and horrible in my bed last night. I couldn't sleep a wink!'

The Queen laughed. 'A true Princess! You've passed!'

Molly chuckled to herself. Those kicks from the donkey had come in useful after all!

6

The Teeny Weeny Tiniest Waists

There were only fifteen princesses left, including Princess Esmeralda and Molly.

It was time for them to put on their ball dresses.

The princesses pushed Molly out of the

way and hogged the mirrors. They used all the make-up. They made the maids brush their hair and iron their dresses again and again.

Molly watched them in amazement. Was this the way real princesses behaved?

'This crown is the latest design,' said Princess Esmeralda. 'It's made of solid gold with diamonds and rubies. It was very expensive. My father had to sell two palaces to buy it.'

'My crown is made of platinum with diamonds and sapphires,' said Princess Snowflake. 'It was a lot more expensive than yours. My father had to sell half his kingdom to buy it.'

Molly put on her own crown. It was pretty. The twisted wire bounced up and down, the polished coloured glass gleamed. Dear Stan, she thought. How kind he is. I do miss him!

'Ooo! That's a cool crown!' said Princess Snowflake.

'So unusual,' said Princess Esmeralda. 'It must have been terribly expensive!'

'It's just a trinket,' said Molly. 'It was made for me by my personal crown designer, Sir Stanley Splendido. My father is so rich he didn't notice the cost.'

'Wow!' said Princess Snowflake. 'I've

heard of Sir Splendido. He's really famous, isn't he?'

'Golly!' said Princess Esmeralda. 'Lucky you!'

Yes, I am, thought Molly. And she felt a little sad. She didn't mean to lie, it had just come out and these silly girls believed anything!

Princess Esmeralda squashed herself into her ball gown.

'I look fat!' she screamed. She measured her middle. 'My waist is forty-seven

centimetres!' she cried. 'That's enormous!
Pull the laces tighter, maid! Tighter!'

The maid pulled and tugged. She couldn't
make Princess Esmeralda's bodice any
smaller.

'Let me,' said Molly. Molly's arms were
strong. She was used to tugging up giant
turnips and digging up stupendous swedes.

Molly braced herself with one foot on

Princess Esmeralda's bottom, the other on the floor. She grabbed the laces and pulled.

'Ahhh! Oh! Eek!' cried Princess Esmeralda. 'I can't breathe. I'm going to faint . . . That looks wonderful!' She measured her waist. 'Thirty-nine centimetres! Brilliant!'

'Do me! Do me!' the other princesses cried.

So Molly laced them all up as tightly as she could.

'Perfect!'

'Heavenly!'

'Are you sure they're not too tight?' asked

Molly. 'I don't want you to fa—'

'Oh be quiet!' the princesses said. 'You're worse than my mother!'

'Just because you don't have such a small waist!'

Molly shrugged. What silly girls!

Molly's dress was perfect. Even though it wasn't as expensive or covered in real diamonds like the other dresses, it was gorgeous. The best she'd ever, ever had . . . thanks to Stan. She felt like a real princess wearing it.

Finally she came to her glass slippers.

They were delicate with high heels. She gently pushed her foot into the first shoe.

Oh no! It was too small! Much too small! Molly was horrified. Ma spent so much money to have specially big ones for my gigantic feet, she thought. And they're still too small!

'Hurry up!' cried the other princesses.

They were decked out with silver ribbon and golden net like Christmas trees. 'Come on!'

They disappeared in a glitter of diamonds and shimmering, fluttering silk.

Molly hobbled after them.

At the top of the stairs a princess had fainted and Molly had to step over her. Halfway down the grand staircase three more princesses lay pale and panting.

I knew those laces were too tight, Molly thought. Serves them right. Only eleven of us left now. The competition is hotting up!

7

The Ball

Molly was so excited. She was going to see the Prince for the first time. Somehow she knew that he would choose her. These princesses were such silly girls. They didn't know anything, not even what a pig looked

like, probably! They couldn't feed
hens. Or dust down donkeys.
The prince wouldn't want
to marry them, what
use would they be?

The ballroom
was enormous.
Molly gazed at
it with wonder.
One hundred
mirrors, bigger
than barn doors,
lined the walls.
Two hundred
candelabras,
like upturned
pitchforks, lit
the room. The floor
was black marble; it
gleamed like a black
cockerel's feathers.

A long table was spread with cakes, meringues, ice cream and strawberries. In the centre was a tower of banana splits, covered in cream and chocolate sauce. There were fifty bottles of fizzy pink soda and fifty of fizzy orange soda.

A band was playing music softly. Suddenly the band changed beat; trumpets heralded the arrival of the Prince.

'His Royal Highness Prince Percy Percival!'

The Prince came down the stairs.

'Ohhh!' cried the princesses.

'Isn't he divine!'

Two princesses swooned.

That takes us down to nine, Molly thought as the swooning princesses were carried out.

Prince Percy Percival wore pink tights.

His red velvet shoes had high heels and very pointy toes. His hair was jet black. His jacket was turquoise with flowers of gold and silver thread.

Molly found herself thinking about Stan and how handsome he looked in his faded blue jacket and straw hat. No, no, no! she told herself. Prince Percy Percival is perfect!

The Prince came down the staircase very carefully – Molly wondered if *his* shoes were too small too.

The Queen and the King introduced him to each of the princesses.

'Hellah,' Prince Percy Percival said. 'Hellah. Delightful to meet yah.'

The Prince was going to dance with each princess and chat to them.

Princess Beautybella, Princess Primrose and Princess Shirley drank ten bottles of pink fizz, ate seven meringues and twelve banana splits and had to be carried out of the ballroom.

Six girls were left.

8

Dirty Dancing

At last it was Molly's turn to dance with
Prince Percy Percival.

'Where did yah go skiing this yar?' the
Prince asked, staring over Molly's shoulder.

'I don't ski,' said Molly, forgetting, for a moment, to lie. 'But I did go skating on Piddledown Pond.'

'I sah, how original!' said the Prince. 'Piddletown Pond, eh? Veh exotic!' He laughed as if she'd told him a very funny joke.

He doesn't know the pond is full of ducks and mud, Molly thought. In fact – she stared at him – I don't think he even knows what a pond is!

Her feet were hurting dreadfully. She was limping and trying not to show it. Nothing was turning out as well as she'd hoped.

'I love dancing!' said the Prince, twirling around. 'It really is spiffing fun, what?'

'Smashing!' Molly said through gritted teeth.

Princess Esmeralda watched Molly and Prince Percy Percival. She thought were getting on rather too well. She didn't like that. As the couple danced by, she flung a banana split at their feet.

'Watch out!' cried Molly.

Prince Percy Percival trod right on the banana skin. His feet slithered out from under him and he crashed to the floor.

The band came to a sudden silence. Everyone watched Prince Percy Percival skid across the floor on his royal bottom. His face was bright red. His black curls got in his eyes.

'How dashed embarrassing!' he was heard to say under his breath as he sailed over the marble.

Molly felt sorry for him.

'Well done, Prince Percy Percival!' she cried running after him. 'That's it! That's exactly what I looked like on the pond!' And she clapped her hands loudly. 'You are a clever mimic! Come on, everyone! A round of applause for the Prince with the most slippery, slidey bottom in the whole kingdom!'

Molly yanked Prince Percy Percival to his feet as if he were a big swede. She dusted him off as if he were the old donkey. The princesses clapped.

'What a great party piece!' Molly said.

'Thenks, oh, yah, thenks!' said the Prince. He winked at Molly. 'You're some gal!' he said. 'You really are. Now, let me tell you all about myself.'

And he did. For hours.

At midnight, the ball came to an end. Molly had spent most of the evening with the Prince. Molly knew a great deal about him, but he had never even asked her name.

Her feet were aching from being squashed into the too small glass slippers. She was tired and feeling lonely.

The other princesses were jealous of the Prince liking Molly and dancing with her all evening. Molly was halfway up the great staircase on her way to bed, when Princess Snowflake gave her a shove.

'Oh sorree!' Princess Snowflake said, grinning.

Molly tripped and lost her shoe. The glass slipper tumbled down the stairs with a tinkling, ringing sound.

Molly ran on without it.

Prince Percy Percival picked it up and kissed it.

9

She Whom the Slipper Fits

In the morning the six remaining princesses gathered to hear which princess the prince had chosen.

None of the other girls were being friendly to Molly.

'Cheat!' hissed Princess Snowflake. 'You put a spell on the Prince to make him like you!'

'Cheat!' said Princess Esmeralda. 'You laced us up so tight we couldn't breathe.'

Molly sat by an open window. She could smell the fresh green smells of the countryside. She could see hills and trees. A donkey brayed. She wiped a tear from her eye. Being a princess was really not much fun.

The doors were flung open. The Queen and Prince Percy Percival came in, followed by a little footman carrying a satin cushion. In the centre of the cushion was Molly's glass slipper.

'Whoever this shoe fits shall be my bride!' cried Prince Percy Percival.

'Me!' cried Princess Snowflake. 'It's mine! I dropped it last night.'

'It was me!' yelled Princess Esmeralda.

'That is my shoe!'

The Queen pointed at Molly. 'Try Princess Blondine first,' she said.

Molly didn't want to try on the slipper. She knew it was hers. But they were all watching, so she slipped off one clog.

'What enormous feet!' cried Princess Esmeralda. 'Yuck!'

'If the shoe fits . . .' said the Queen.

The footman knelt down and tried to put the shoe onto Molly's foot. It would not fit. He tried to fold and bend the foot and force it into the shoe. But Molly stuck out her toes. The shoe would not go on; it was too small.

'Now that's a shame!' said the Queen. 'I like the gal! Push a little. Tug a bit! Tuck your toes in, gal.'

But Molly didn't want to. She wouldn't even try.

She stood up and threw the shoe to

Princess Esmeralda. 'It's yours!' she said. 'You have the Prince. You two are much better suited. I could never marry someone who never looked at me or knew my name. I'm off!'

'Well really!' Prince Percy Percival said. 'Who's that rude gal?'

Molly leaped through the open window. 'Goodbye!' she called.

She landed in an old cart full of bags of corn and nails and broken horseshoes. The donkey pulling it brayed. The young man in the blue jacket turned round and helped her onto the seat beside him.

'Hello, Stan,' said Molly.

'Hello, my princess,' said Stan.

Hello my princess

By the same author

ᴛʜᴇ DOG ɪɴ ᴛʜᴇ DIAMOND COLLAR

by Rebecca Lisle

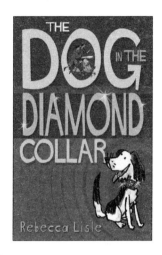

'A proper story,
entertainingly
observed.'
SUNDAY TIMES

*Not many stray dogs roam the streets wearing
diamond collars . . . But Clinky Monkey does.
How is Clinky Monkey connected to the kidnapped boy,
Timothy Potts-Smythe? Why does the butler lie? Why does
the ransom note stink so badly?
Who is hiding in the zoo?*

*Three brothers have a hilarious adventure involving bears, a
boy and a big gorilla as they try to solve the mystery of . . .
THE DOG IN THE DIAMOND COLLAR.*

ᴛʜᴇ DOG ɪɴ ᴛʜᴇ DIAMOND COLLAR

£4.99 ISBN 9781842703663

By the same author

THE BOY IN THE BIG BLACK BOX

by Rebecca Lisle

*Another funny mystery adventure for Joe, Laurie and
Theo (helped by Clinky Monkey, of course) follows*
THE DOG IN THE DIAMOND COLLAR

*Ivor Trick's magic show goes wrong when Wee Willie
walks into the big Disappearing Box – and vanishes.
Ivor blames Daphne Davorski. She blames Ivor.
Spells fly. Tempers rage.
Where is the BOY IN THE BIG BLACK BOX?*

THE BOY IN THE BIG BLACK BOX

£4.99   ISBN 9781842706817

THE TOAD PRINCE

by Rebecca Lisle

'A witty take on
The Frog Prince,
in which the
princess can't
resist a suitor
who eats worms
and flies.'
SUNDAY TIMES

*Trevor the Toad is in love with Princess Petunia,
but warty brown toads don't marry princesses —
unless there's a bit of magic involved. Evil Wizard
Wazp usually turns frogs into princes, but when his
clever dog Pong suggests he turns a TOAD into a
prince, he takes up the magical challenge. Anything
to impress the King!*

*What Wazp doesn't know is that clever Pong has
toadally tricked him . . .*

THE TOAD PRINCE

£4.99 ISBN 1842703153